Littlest Snowman

by Rita Walsh
illustrated by Jenny Williams

Watermill Press

Printed in the United States of America.

10 9 8 7 6 5 4 3 2 1

Once upon a time there was a little snowman. He had round little cheeks and a chubby little tummy. And on top of his head he wore a little striped hat with a brightly colored pom-pom.

Late one night, when all the girls and boys in town were asleep, the North Wind began to blow. It blew around the little snowman and swept his little hat away!

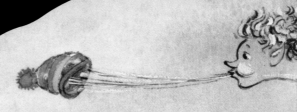

"Oh, no!" cried the snowman as his hat blew this way and that.

His snowmen friends saw the little snowman chasing his hat.

"We'll help you!" they said.

Soon all the snowmen were
chasing the hat. But the North
Wind was faster than any of them.
It blew the hat right out of town!

The little snowmen went sliding
past a farm.

"We'll help you!" called the
horses. So the snowmen hopped
into the sleighs and took off.

But the North Wind blew even harder. The horses galloped out of the pasture, down a little path, and into the woods.

Some little birds woke up
when they heard all the noise.
"We'll help you!" they chirped.

By now, there was quite a group chasing after the little snowman's hat. But no matter how hard they tried, they just couldn't catch up with the North Wind.

"It's no use," said the little
snowman, watching his hat swirl
through the trees.

"Don't give up!" said the horses
and the birds.

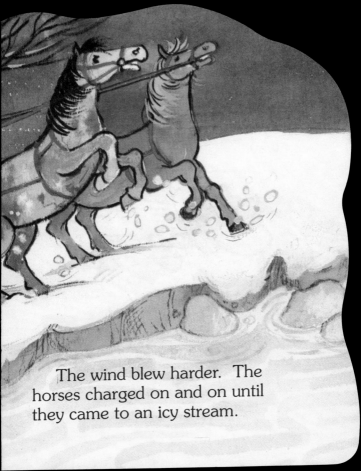

The wind blew harder. The
horses charged on and on until
they came to an icy stream.

"Now what do we do?" asked
the snowmen.

The little snowman watched
as his hat blew farther and farther
away.

"I'm tired," said the little snowman. "That old North Wind can keep my hat. Let's go home."

When the North Wind heard that,
he got very upset. He didn't want to
stop playing with the snowmen and
the horses and the birds.

"I'm sorry," said the North Wind. "I wasn't trying to be mean. I just wanted to play."

The little snowman and his friends were very surprised. "We'd love to play with you!" they told the North Wind.

The new friends played
all night in the snowy woods.
Everyone danced while the North
Wind whistled a tune. What a
wonderful time they had!

When the night was over, the North Wind gently blew the birds back to their nests, and the horses back to their pasture, and the sleepy snowmen back to their little town.

And before he blew back up to the clouds, the North Wind very gently blew the striped hat with the pom-pom—right back onto the little snowman's head!